LAUGH-OUT-LOUD JOKES

LAUGH-OUT-LOUD HISTORY JOKES

CAITIE MCANENEY

WINDMILL BOOKS

Published in 2025 by Windmill Books, an Imprint of Rosen Publishing
2544 Clinton St., Buffalo, NY 14224

First Edition

Editor: Caitie McAneney
Book Design: Claire Zimmermann

Photo Credits: Cover, p.1 (child) Luis Molinero/Shutterstock.com; cover, p. 4, 20, 22, 23 (book, clock, and vase illustrations) Look_Studio/Shutterstock.com; cover, pp. 6, 10, 12, (car, knight, carriage, coat of arms, and airplane illustrations) Macrovector/Shutterstock.com; cover, p. 14 (Colosseum illustration) NeutronStar8/Shutterstock.com; cover, p. 18 (scroll illustrations) IGORdeyka/Shutterstock.com; cover, p. 8 (ship illustration) Mind Pixell/Shutterstock.com; series art (paper texture) OanaGherghe2/Shutterstock.com; p. 5 EnricoAliberti ItalyPhoto/Shutterstock.com; p. 7 Kozlik/Shutterstock.com; p. 9 vlastas/Shutterstock.com; p. 11 Songquan Deng/Shutterstock.com; p. 13 courtesy of the Library of Congress; p. 15 Richard Panasevich/Shutterstock.com; p. 17 Miro Varcek/Shutterstock.com; p. 19 Joseph Karl Stieler's Beethoven mit dem Manuskript der Missa solemnis.jpg/Wikimedia Commons; p. 21 Tyler Olson/Shutterstock.com.

Library of Congress Cataloging-in-Publication Data

Names: McAneney, Caitie, author.
Title: Laugh-out-loud history jokes / Caitie McAneney.
Description: Buffalo : Windmill Books, 2025. | Series: Laugh-out-loud jokes | Includes index.
Identifiers: LCCN 2024008327 (print) | LCCN 2024008328 (ebook) | ISBN 9781538396803 (library binding) | ISBN 9781538396797 (paperback) | ISBN 9781538396810 (ebook)
Subjects: LCSH: History–Juvenile humor.
Classification: LCC PN6231.H47 M325 2025 (print) | LCC PN6231.H47 (ebook) | DDC 808 88/2–dc23/eng/20240306
LC record available at https://lccn.loc.gov/2024008327
LC ebook record available at https://lccn.loc.gov/2024008328

Manufactured in the United States of America

CPSIA Compliance Information: Batch #CSWM25. For further information, contact Rosen Publishing at 1-800-237-9932

CONTENTS

Words in the glossary appear in **bold** the first time they are used in the text.

ANCIENT JOKES

What did kids watch in ancient Greece?

TROY STORY.

How did the Roman Empire split?

WITH A PAIR OF CAESARS.

Why didn't the Egyptian go to the doctor when he was hurt?

HE WAS IN DE-NILE.

Why was the pharoah scared?

HE LOST HIS MUMMY!

FUN FACT!

Troy was a city known as the setting of the ancient Greek **myth** of the Trojan War.

Julius Caesar, Roman leader

KNIGHT HUMOR

Where did the knight park his camel?

IN THE CAMEL-LOT.

Why was King Arthur so tired?

HE HAD TO WORK THE KNIGHT SHIFT.

What did the knight's grave say?

RUST IN PEACE.

Why was it so dark in the Dark Ages?

THERE WERE SO MANY KNIGHTS.

FUN FACT!

King Arthur was a **legendary** person in **medieval** British tales. Legend said he had a group of knights who met around his Round Table.

ON THE HIGH SEAS

Where do pirates love to sail to?

ARRRGENTINA.

Why did explorers cross the ocean?

TO GET TO THE OTHER TIDE.

How did Vikings talk to each other?

THEY USED **NORSE** CODE.

What did the ocean say to the pirate?

NOTHING AT ALL. IT JUST WAVED!

FUN FACT!

Vikings were also called Norsemen. They were warriors from Northern Europe who sailed the seas and took land.

EARLY AMERICA

What do you get when you cross a dog and an American **patriot**?

A YANKEE POODLE.

What happened when the Liberty Bell heard a joke?

IT CRACKED UP!

Where was the Declaration of Independence signed?

AT THE BOTTOM.

What did the patriots wear to the Boston Tea Party?

TEA-SHIRTS.

FUN FACT!

The Liberty Bell sits across the street from Independence Hall in Philadelphia, Pennsylvania.

FAMOUS FIGURES

Why didn't King George like the American colonies?

HE THOUGHT THEY WERE REVOLTING.

What did Benjamin Franklin say when he discovered electricity?

"I'M SHOCKED!"

Two wrongs don't make a right. But what can two Wrights make?

AN AIRPLANE.

Why did King Arthur have a round table?

HE DIDN'T LIKE TO BE CORNERED!

FUN FACT!

In 1752, Benjamin Franklin is believed to have flown a kite with a key on it into a thunderstorm to explore the connection between lightning and electricity.

SILLY SITUATIONS

Why didn't Plato like his French fries?

THEY WERE MADE IN ANCIENT GREASE.

What did the pharoah say when he entered his pyramid?

"MUMMY'S HOME!"

What do you call a Roman leader with a head cold?

JULIUS SNEEZER.

Why did the mummy need a spa day?

HE WAS ALL WOUND UP.

FUN FACT!

Plato was a famous **philosopher** from ancient Greece.

WHAT DO YOU GET?

What do you get when you cross a pharoah and a trumpet?

TOOTING-KHAMUN.

What do you get when you cross a Roman and a vegetable garden?

A CAESAR SALAD.

What food did the pharoah order?

PIZZA TUT!

What do you get when you cross a knight and a rabbit?

SIR HOP-A-LOT.

FUN FACT!

Tutankhamen, also called King Tut, was an ancient Egyptian pharoah who came to power when he was only nine years old.

MUSIC ON THE MIND

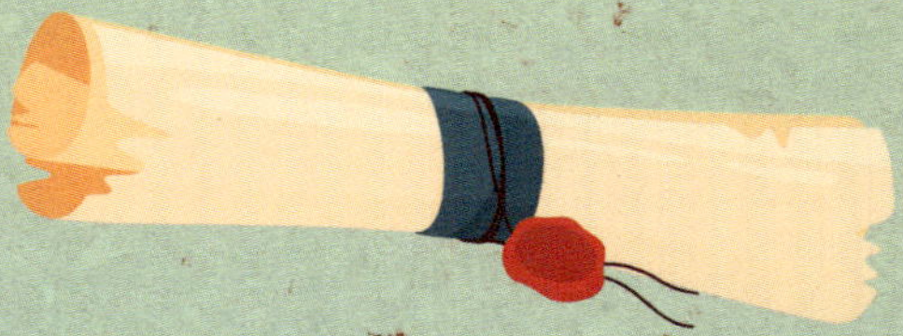

What kind of music do mummies like?

WRAP MUSIC.

What did the Pilgrims listen to?

PLYMOUTH ROCK.

Why did the colonists need music?

THEY WERE FIGHTING FOR INDEPEN-DANCE.

Why didn't Beethoven like chickens?

ALL THEY EVER TALKED ABOUT WAS "BACH, BACH, BACH."

FUN FACT!

Johann Sebastian Bach and Ludwig van Beethoven were both great German **composers.**

Ludwig van Beethoven

STUDYING HISTORY

What did the snake study in school?

HISSSSSTORY.

What do history teachers like to talk about?

THE GOOD OLD DAYS.

Why didn't the college student get a degree in history?

SHE COULDN'T SEE A FUTURE IN IT.

What's the sweetest subject in school?

HISTORY, BECAUSE IT'S FULL OF DATES!

FUN FACT!

History is the period in the past in which events were recorded. The time before written records is called prehistory.

GLOSSARY

ancient: Very old.

composer: Someone who writes music.

legendary: Having to do with a story handed down from the past that is popularly accepted but cannot be checked.

medieval: Having to do with the Middle Ages, a time in European history from about 500 to 1500 CE.

myth: A story that was told by a people to explain a practice, belief, or natural event.

Norse: Relating to ancient Norway.

patriot: An American colonist who wanted independence from England.

pharoah: A ruler of ancient Egypt.

philosopher: A person who tries to discover and to understand the nature of knowledge.

revolting: Disgusting. Also, rebelling.

Yankee: A native of the United States.

FOR MORE INFORMATION

BOOKS

Bryant, Chuck, and Josh Clark. *Stuff Kids Should Know: The Mind-Blowing Histories of (Almost) Everything.* New York, NY: Henry Holt and Company, 2023.

Levy, Janey. *The Marvels of Ancient Egypt.* New York, NY: Gareth Stevens Publishing, 2022.

Redshaw, Hermione. *A Kid's Life in Ancient Egypt.* Minneapolis, MN: Bearport Publishing Company, 2023.

WEBSITES

Social Studies
jr.brainpop.com/socialstudies/
Explore fun facts about history with BrainPop.

10 Facts About Ancient Rome
www.natgeokids.com/uk/discover/history/romans/10-facts-about-the-ancient-romans/
Discover 10 fun facts about life in the time of ancient Rome!

Publisher's note to educators and parents: Our editors have carefully reviewed these websites to ensure that they are suitable for students. Many websites change frequently, however, and we cannot guarantee that a site's future contents will continue to meet our high standards of quality and educational value. Be advised that students should be closely supervised whenever they access the internet.

INDEX